For information address Disney Press,
1101 Flower Street, Glendale, California 91201.

Printed in China
First Edition
3 5 7 9 10 8 6 4 2
ISBN 978-1-4847-0279-6
T425-2382-5-14356

For more Disney Press fun, visit www.disneybooks.com
This book was printed on paper created from a sustainable source.

DISNEY PRINCESS

Aurora and the Diamond Crown

Disney PRESS

New York • Los Angeles

Aurora awoke one sunny morning in the most cheerful of moods. After all, it was her seventeenth birthday, and she could not wait to see what wonderful surprises were in store.

Luckily, she did not have to wait too long. As soon as she had gotten dressed, her mother, the Queen, came in.

"Happy birthday, darling," said the Queen.

Aurora was quick to notice that her mother was wearing a crown Aurora had never seen before. Gleaming at its center was a large pink heart-shaped diamond trimmed all around with tiny sparkling diamonds.

"Mother!" she cried. "What a beautiful crown! Is it new?"

"Actually," replied the Queen, "it's quite old. And it's the reason that I've come to you so early on this very special day."

The Queen took Aurora by
the hand and led her to a great portrait hall.

"Why, Mother!" exclaimed Aurora, pointing to the nearest portrait.
"Is that you?"

"Indeed, it is," replied the Queen. "It was painted on my seventeenth birthday. You see,
Aurora, it's a tradition in our kingdom that on a princess's seventeenth birthday, this crown
is to be passed down to her by her mother."

"Oh, Mother!" Aurora gasped. "Is that crown truly to be mine?"

"Well," her mother said with a smile, "I certainly hope so! *But,* according to tradition, you must first earn it."

"How?" asked Aurora.

"By answering three riddles," her mother explained.

Just then, the three good fairies, Flora, Fauna, and Merryweather, flew in.

"Happy birthday, Princess!" said Merryweather. "We're here to give you your clues!"

Then the Queen kissed Aurora. "Think hard, my dear. And good luck!"

With a wave of their magic wands, the fairies made themselves bigger and transported themselves and Aurora out onto the castle grounds. Then Flora stepped up and recited the first riddle:

"To the eyes, it's a treat; to the nose, a delight.
But beware! To the hand it can be quite a fright.
Though few think to taste it, its sweetness still shows.
To this first riddle, the answer's a . . ."

"Hmmm . . ." said Aurora when Flora was done.

"Oh! I know!" said Merryweather.

"Of course you know," scolded Fauna. "It's Aurora who has to guess!"

"Do you know what the answer is, dearie?" asked Flora.

"Let's see," said Aurora. "'To the eyes, it's a treat.' So it's pretty. . . . 'To the nose, a delight.' So it smells good. . . . 'To the hand . . . quite a fright.' So it must hurt . . . like a thorn . . . on a rose. That's it, isn't it?" And she hurried off to the rose garden, where she picked the biggest, most fragrant rose she could find.

"Very good!" exclaimed Fauna. "And now for the second one:

Some plant it, some steal it, some blow it away.
Some do it several times in a day.
Some who are shy might blush getting this
On their hand or their cheek. Can you guess? It's a . . ."

"Well . . ." said Aurora, thinking. "If 'some plant it,'
it might be another flower—a dandelion, perhaps?
You can blow them away, too. Of course, we
don't have any of those in our garden. But what
can you get on your hand or your cheek . . . ?"
she wondered aloud as she gazed at her
reflection in the garden pool.

"I know!" Aurora cried suddenly. "It's a kiss, isn't it? Of course it is!" And, as if to prove it, she planted a kiss on each of the fairies, causing them to blush.

"Honestly," said Flora, "you're figuring out the answers more quickly than any princess yet!"

"Now it's my turn!" exclaimed Merryweather. "Are you ready, Aurora?"

"I think so," she replied.

"Ahem." Merryweather cleared her throat.

"What only gets stronger the longer it lives?
What pays you back tenfold the more that you give?
Some say it's blind, some say it's true,
Some just say simply, 'I . . . feel this . . . for you.'"
Merryweather giggled. "Silly me!
I almost said the answer!"

"Well, let's see," said Aurora. "It might be a tree. That 'gets stronger the longer it lives.' And I suppose you could say that a tree is blind. But so are bats. . . ."

Aurora thought and thought. She was still thinking when Prince Phillip walked by, leading his horse, Samson.

"Happy birthday, my love!" he called with a big smile.

And instantly, Aurora knew what the answer to the riddle was.

Happily, Aurora hurried back to the castle and up to her mother's sewing room.

"I've solved the riddles!" she announced. She took the pink rose from her hair and handed it to the Queen. Then Aurora gave her mother a kiss on the cheek.

"Very good!" declared the Queen. "And the answer to the third riddle?"

That was when the fairies brought in Prince Phillip.

"It's *love*," said Aurora, "of course!"

No sooner had Aurora said the word than the Queen took the crown from her head and proudly placed it on Aurora's. (And then, some say, the heart-shaped diamond shone even brighter than before!)

That very afternoon, Aurora
had her portrait painted, just as
all the clever princesses who had
come before her had.

And that night there was a grand birthday ball held in the castle in Aurora's honor.

"Happy birthday, Aurora, my darling," her mother warmly told her. "And may you have many, many more!"